Gertie Gorilla's Glorious Gift

by Barbara deRubertis • illustrated by R.W. Alley

THE KANE PRESS / NEW YORK

P9-DXL-261

Alpha Betty's Class

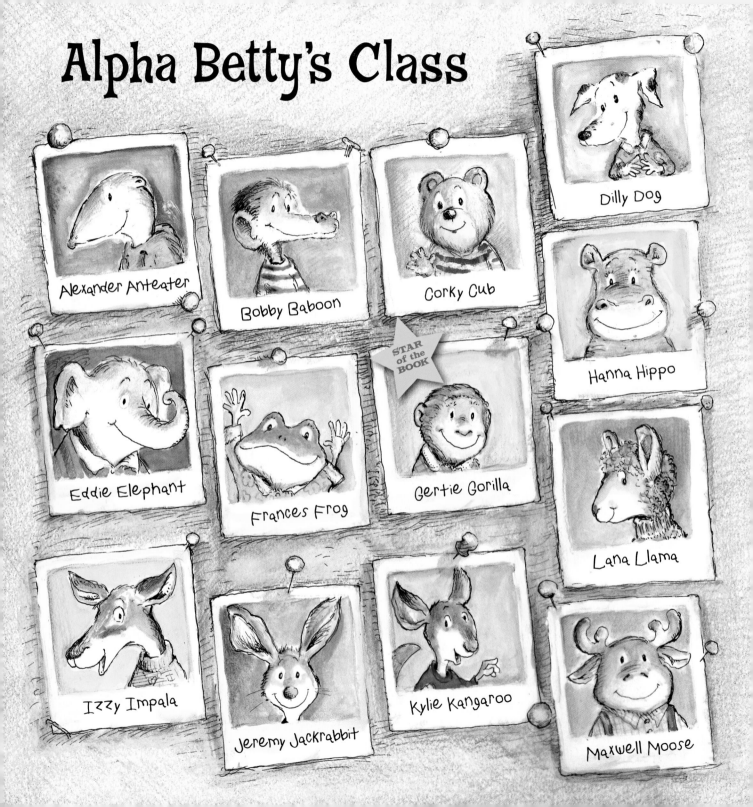

Alexander Anteater

Bobby Baboon

Corky Cub

Dilly Dog

Eddie Elephant

Frances Frog

STAR of the BOOK

Gertie Gorilla

Hanna Hippo

Lana Llama

Izzy Impala

Jeremy Jackrabbit

Kylie Kangaroo

Maxwell Moose

Library of Congress Cataloging-in-Publication Data

deRubertis, Barbara.
Gertie Gorilla's glorious gift / by Barbara deRubertis ; illustrated by R.W. Alley.
p. cm. — (Animal antics A to Z)
Summary: When Gertie Gorilla gets muddy on her way to Godfrey Goat's birthday
party, her gazelle friend suggests she clean up in a nearby brook but worries what
will happen to her grubby gift.
ISBN 978-1-57565-318-1 (library binding : alk. paper) — ISBN 978-1-57565-311-2 (pbk. : alk. paper)
[1. Gifts—Fiction. 2. Birthdays—Fiction. 3. Gorilla—Fiction. 4. Gazelles—Fiction. 5. Goats—Fiction.
6. Alphabet. 7. Humorous stories.] I. Alley, R. W. (Robert W.), ill. II. Title.
PZ7.D4475Ger 2010
[E]—dc22   2009049882

1 3 5 7 9 10 8 6 4 2

First published in the United States of America in 2010 by Kane Press, Inc.
Printed in the United States of America
WOZ0710

Series Editor: Juliana Hanford
Book Design: Edward Miller

Animal Antics A to Z is a registered trademark of Kane Press, Inc.

www.kanepress.com

Gertie Gorilla hurried home from Alpha Betty's school.

Today she was going to Godfrey Goat's birthday party!

Gertie gathered everything she needed
to wrap her gift for Godfrey.

She had glossy paper.
She had glittery bows.

And she had a goofy card.
It was sure to make Godfrey giggle!

Soon Gertie was finished.
She gazed at her gift.
It was glorious!

Godfrey would gasp with glee
when she gave it to him.

Gertie said goodbye to Gramps and Granny.

She galloped across the garden.
She wiggled through the gate.
And she waggled past the grove
of green trees.

Gertie gazed up at the leaves.

"Golly!" she grinned.
"I just got a great idea!

I'll grab a vine and GLIDE over
that grubby gulch."

As Gertie was gliding over the gulch,
she gasped!

The vine sagged. It groaned.
And then it gave way.

"Going! Going! GONE!" cried Gertie.

She hit the ground with a gooey *ga-lumph*.

She got a grimy bath in grubby grit.

And she lost her grip on Godfrey's gift!

The gift hit the bottom of the soggy,
boggy gulch.

"Oh, NOOOOO!" Gertie groaned.
"Godfrey's gift is a goner.
And LOOK at my gorgeous gown!"

Gertie struggled out of the gulch.

Just then Gary Gazelle came
galloping up the hill.

"Gertie!" cried Gary.
"Where are you going in such
a grubby gown?"

Then he gasped. "And LOOK at
that grimy gift down in the gulch!"

"I WAS going to Godfrey Goat's birthday party," Gertie grumbled.

"But now I can't go.
My gift and I are too grubby!"

Gary grinned. He led Gertie to
the other side of the hill.

"I suggest that you jump in
this nice, clean gurgling brook.

You'll be a bit soggy.
But you won't be grubby!"

"That's a great idea!" said Gertie.

She wiggled and waggled her way
down to the gushing brook.

Bing! Bang! BOING!

Gertie flung herself into the water.

Gertie was giddy with glee.

She giggled as she wiggled in
the gurgling brook.

She plunged under the water.

"Golly, that felt GOOD!" Gertie gulped.

Then Gertie Gorilla groaned.

"But what should I do about
my grimy gift?"

Gary brought the gift to Gertie.

"You can't wash it," said Gary.
"Your gift would be too soggy!"

Suddenly Gertie grinned.
She grabbed the gift.
She hugged it tightly.

And then she plunged under
the water again.

Glug! Glug! Glug!

"Oh, NO!" gasped Gary.
"Your gift is soaking wet!"

"Oh, YES!" giggled Gertie.
"Water won't hurt THIS gift."

The dripping gift glistened
in the golden sunlight.

It gleamed and glowed,
just like Gertie.

Gary Gazelle groaned.
"What will you tell Godfrey
about his soggy gift?"

Gertie Gorilla grinned.
"I'll tell Godfrey the truth.
His gift is ready to go!"

When Gertie galloped into Godfrey's
party, she handed him the drippy gift.

"It's a little soggy," she giggled.
"But water is GOOD for this gift!"

Godfrey tore off the drippy paper.
He opened the soggy box.

"Oh, Gertie!" he gasped.
"What a great gift!
SWIM GOGGLES!"

Gertie grinned happily.

Then Godfrey Goat grabbed Gertie
Gorilla's hand.

And together they galloped with glee
into the gurgling brook!

STAR OF THE BOOK: THE GORILLA

FUN FACTS
- Home: In mountains and forests near the equator in Africa
- Size: Gorillas are the largest of all the apes. Males usually weigh about 400 pounds, but females weigh less.
- Favorite foods: Fruit, leaves, vines, roots, and tree bark
- Bedtime: Gorillas build nests on the ground for sleeping. Young gorillas also like to sleep in trees.
- **Did You Know?** Gorillas are usually quiet and shy, but they will roar and beat their chests to chase away strangers. Yikes!

LOOK BACK
Learning to identify letter sounds (phonemes) at the beginning, middle, and end of words is called "phonemic awareness."

- The word *gift* begins with the *g* sound. Listen to the words on page 6 being read again. When you hear a word that begins with the *g* sound, hold your hands up high and wiggle your fingers while you make three *g* sounds: *g-g-g*!
- The word *wiggle* has a *g* sound in the middle! Listen to the words on page 20 being read again. When you hear a word that has the *g* sound in the middle, put your hands in front of your chest and wiggle your fingers while you make three *g* sounds: *g-g-g*!

TRY THIS!
Stand Up, Sit Down for G Sounds!
- Listen to the words in the box below being read aloud.
- When you hear a word that begins with the *g* sound, stand up.
- When you hear a word that ends with the *g* sound, sit down.
- If you hear a word that begins AND ends with the *g* sound, stand up and then sit down!

gift	tag	gorilla	big
glug	goat	bug	game
hug	gag	good	bag

FOR MORE ACTIVITIES, go to Gertie Gorilla's website: www.kanepress.com/AnimalAntics/GertieGorilla.html
You'll also find a recipe for Gertie Gorilla's Glorious Glazed Carrots!